Hi Ho! Here's a good book!

THIS BOOK BELONGS TO
SAMANTHA ZAWALICH

© Henson Associates, Inc. 1981, 1989

Love,
Aunt Susan
Christmas
1996

WENDY WASSERSTEIN

PAMELA'S FIRST MUSICAL

ILLUSTRATED BY
ANDREW JACKNESS

Hyperion / New York

Special thanks to:
Al Hirschfeld, Andre Bishop,
Gerald Gutierrez, Michael Lynton,
Ethel Merman, Mary Martin,
and Luis Sanjurjo

Text © 1996 by Wendy Wasserstein.
Illustrations © 1996 by Andrew Jackness.

Playbill is a registered trademark of Playbill, Inc.

Printed in Singapore.
FIRST EDITION
1 3 5 7 9 10 8 6 4 2
The artwork for each picture is prepared using gouache.
This book is set in 14-point Palatino.

Library of Congress Cataloging-in-Publication Data

Wasserstein, Wendy.
Pamela's first musical / written by Wendy Wasserstein ;
illustrated by Andrew Jackness. — 1st ed.   p.   cm.
Summary: Pamela has the best birthday ever when her glamorous Aunt Louise takes her
to see a Broadway musical.
ISBN 0-7868-0078-X (trade)—ISBN 0-7868-2063-2 (lib. bdg.)
[1. Musicals—Fiction. 2. Aunts—Fiction. 3. Birthdays— Fiction.] I. Jackness, Andrew, ill. II. Title.
PZ7.W2588Pam   1996
[Fic]—dc20   95-36133

For Pamela
—W. W.

For my mother
—A. J.

O n Saturday morning Pamela woke up extra-extra early.

"Today is my birthday," she said to her favorite dolls as she gathered them into her bed for a chat. "I'm nine. And nine means a lot when you're eight. It means I'm almost ten. And ten means I'm almost old enough to drive or be a movie star."

"Well, if it was my birthday," Barbie said, tugging at her fuzzy pink negligee, "I'd wish that Ken would give me a new car, ruby earrings, and a mink skating outfit. What will you wish for, Pamela?"

Pamela took a deep breath. "Well, first I'd wish that on my birthday all wars would stop and all the children on earth had enough food to eat forever." Lola, Pamela's dancing cat, waltzed around the room.

"And then," continued Pamela, "I'd wish for an Electronic Magic Diary, the Easy-to-Do Creepy Crawlers Jewelry Set, a Winter Princess Barbie, and I-wish-I-wish-I-wish I get to see my aunt Louise. My aunt Louise is a perfectly perfect person. We always have a most splendiferous time!"

"Pamela, time for breakfast." Her father's voice interrupted the conversation. Immediately Pamela leaped out of bed, put on her best party dress, and raced down the stairs so that her birthday could officially begin.

As soon as Pamela came into the kitchen, her mother turned out the lights and everybody—including Lola—sang "Happy Birthday." Then Pamela unwrapped an Electronic Magic Diary from her father, a Winter Princess Barbie from her mother, and a six-foot blow-up yellow stegosaurus that her brother, Daniel, had selected and secretly hoped he could keep for himself.

"We also have a special surprise for you, Pamela." Her mother smiled. "Today Aunt Louise is going to take you to see a Broadway musical."

"Yuck!" Daniel slammed down his orange juice. Daniel only liked "really cool scary movies" with *Halloween* or *Friday the Thirteenth* in the title.

Just then Aunt Louise pulled into the driveway in her red sports coupe. She honked the horn. "Oooooooh, dahling, I'm here!" Aunt Louise said "oooooooh, dahling" all the time. It drove Pamela's daddy bananas.

Pamela jumped into the car and waved good-bye to her mother, her father, Daniel, and Lola. She was off to New York City with her favorite aunt to see a musical. All of Pamela's friends at school knew grown-ups who went into the city every day to work. But Pamela's aunt Louise actually *lived* there.

"Hello there, young lady." Nick the doorman tipped his hat to Pamela the moment she arrived at her aunt's apartment house. "Cold enough for you?" Pamela liked Nick. He was always friendly and knew all about the weather.

Aunt Louise quickly changed out of her driving clothes into her theater clothes. She had a different outfit for every occasion. In fact, whenever Pamela visited, Aunt Louise would invite her to walk right into her closet and try on a few ensembles herself.

Just then a dashing man came to their table and kissed Aunt Louise's hand.

"Bear, this is my niece Pamela." Aunt Louise was blushing. "Pamela, this is Bearish Nureyjinksy, the world-famous dancer."

"A pleasure." He did a grand tour jeté leap all the way back to his table.

The blini arrived. They were just like pancakes. And the tea came in a glass with little cherries on the bottom.

"Oooooooh, dahling," Aunt Louise said, looking at her wristwatch. "It's almost curtain time."

Aunt Louise paid the bill, got their coats from the checkroom, and hailed a taxi all in one breath.

KITTIES 4 EVER

45 ST THEATRE

THE PRINCE OF BROADWAY

RUN DON'T WALK
JOE L. SEAGULL

WINNER 17 TONY AWARDS

I LOVED IT! JOHN SIMON

THE BEST PLAY OF THIS OR ANY OTHER SEASON!!

THE BEST SHOW YOU WILL EVER SEE NYT.

...LESSLY FUN

WINNER OUTER LIMITS CRITICS AWARD

SOLD OUT!

When Pamela first saw Broadway, it looked so exciting she thought she had made it all up. She was thrilled when her taxi stopped right in the middle of it all, directly in front of the Forty-fifth Street Theatre.

. . . overture."

Ginger married Prince Billy with fifty tapping bridesmaids, fifty leaping men, the trapeze artists, the dancing cats, Chita and her fastest legs, and a reprise of Pamela's favorite song. Then the red velvet curtain came down.

"Bravo! Bravissimo!" The entire audience was on its feet, applauding.

"It's a standing ovation, just as I'd hoped." Aunt Louise was just thrilled that Pamela's first musical had gone so well.

"Would you like to go backstage and meet Mary Ethel Bernadette?" Aunt Louise asked Pamela as they walked up the aisle.

"You know her?"

"Oooooooh, dahling." Aunt Louise grinned. "I make her blue jeans."

There was so much activity backstage that Pamela didn't know where to look. There was one man running up and down with wigs, a woman with piles of laundry, and Nathan Hines Klines in his undershirt.

A very thin man in blue jeans and a jeans jacket nodded at Aunt Louise. "Mary Ethel Bernadette's dressing room is at the end of the hall." Then he took Pamela's hand. "I'm Harrison Roy, the stage manager. My job is to make certain everything runs smoothly backstage."

"Oooooooh, dahling; you were mahvelous!" Aunt Louise embraced Mary Ethel Bernadette. The only place Pamela had seen as many flowers as she saw in Mary Ethel Bernadette's dressing room was at the botanical gardens.

At first Pamela didn't know what to say. Then she whispered, "This was my first musical, and I loved it. Thank you."

Mary Ethel Bernadette hugged Pamela very tight. "That's the nicest thing anyone could say."

As they were leaving the theater, the old stage door man waved to Pamela to come stand onstage in the empty house. "This is the ghost light," he explained. "This means the theater always stays lit for all the people who ever performed here. It also means you can come back anytime."

That night Pamela gathered all her dolls and the yellow stegosaurus on her bed.

"Now, you'll be Mary Ethel Bernadette, and you'll be Nathan Hines Klines, and I'll be all the other parts."

Lola the dancing cat jumped on the bed. "Lola, you can be everybody else and, of course, all the cats."

Pamela put her Electronic Magic Diary on the bed. It was now a stage.

Pamela slowly dimmed the lights and then lifted a pencil and struck up the orchestra.

That night when her mother and father came in to check on her they thought that Pamela had fallen asleep. But they were wrong.

She wasn't asleep. Pamela was producing, writing, choreographing, designing, and directing hundreds of dancing girls, parades of tapping men, Mary Ethel Bernadette, Nathan Hines Klines, Bearish Nureyjinsky, Aunt Louise, the taxi driver, and a cast of thousands, maybe millions.

And as the red velvet curtain fell,
Pamela took a bow in the greatest,
biggest most splendiferous musical ever.

THE END